The Night
Of The Shooting Stars

The Night Of The Shooting Stars

AN INTERGALACTIC

SCIENCE-FICTION STORY

Evelyn Malacrida Rocco

Full Court Press
Englewood Cliffs, New Jersey

THIS BOOK IS DEDICATED TO

my husband, Frank Rocco
and my son, David Malacrida,
for their love and support,

and to Alex and Andrea Cercone, Ann Schull,
and my family, friends, and former students,
with my gratitude and love.

CHAPTER 1

How It All Began

JESSE LOVES TO LOOK AT THE NIGHT SKY. He never tires of gazing at all those twinkling stars. This fascination has been with him for as long as he can remember.

But Nanney, his adopted mother, watches her dear son very intently as he searches the sky, as if looking for some secret message, searching but not knowing what he's looking for.

He loves his home. Hawaii is such a beautiful place, most especially his island—world-renowned for its deep blue water, gorgeous palm trees, vegetation, and magnificent waterfalls. He can't imagine any place in this world—or, for that matter, *out* of it—being so beautiful.

Jesse is a rather tall, good-looking young man with brown, shoulder-length hair bleached by the tropical sun. He wears an unusual necklace with an exquisite pendant shimmering against his well-tanned chest. Invariably smiling and full of fun, he has a wonderful manner about him that makes people enjoy his company.

This great personality is due, in part, to the loving care of Nanney.

Some years ago, he found out that his family had been vacationing in Hawaii and staying at Nanney's guest house when, one morning, they decided to take a helicopter tour of the island and asked her to babysit. . .but they never returned!

They were eventually declared missing in a helicopter accident. Nanney told Jesse that no close family or relatives of his could be located. As a result, she was able to adopt him.

A rather full-figured woman, she's generally in the habit of laughing and hugging a lot; a good-natured woman, everyone in town is fond of her. She loves wearing brightly colored muu-muu dresses with a beautiful flower in her dark hair, which is always pulled back in a tight bun.

She calls out to Jesse to get ready for tomorrow. Tomorrow is another adventurous day of exploring and wondering. It will be exciting for Lani and him. They will meet at their secret cove to swim and explore the beauty of the reef.

LANI IS HIS BEST FRIEND. She is shorter than Jesse, with large, twinkling brown eyes and long, silky dark hair set off by a beautiful flower. He likes her because she is as energetic, spontaneous, and adventurous as he is.

Lani has always felt there was something very special about him. She has been drawn to him from the very moment they first met at school. They became instant friends, and their friendship has grown each year, just as they have.

This afternoon, after being in that hot classroom, they race to the beach and jump into the waves, clothes and all. They love to surf. Imagine the exhilaration they feel as they catch a perfect wave and ride it into shore! You would have to do it for yourself to feel its awesome power.

Then they lie in the sun, fantasizing about the world they live in and speculating about the ones that might exist somewhere "out there" beyond their planet.

"Jesse, do you think there's really life on other planets?" she asks.

"I don't know—but I've always thought there was *something* else besides stars up there."

"You've always had this intense interest in outer space. Do you think that maybe someday you might become an astronaut?" Lani asks.

"Hey," he says, "that's not a bad idea! Would you miss me if I flew to another galaxy?"

"Well, maybe for a little while, or until another cutie came along!" she says teasingly.

But they soon pack up and head out—it's time to go home and face the real world.

For a special birthday, Nanney bought him a magnificent telescope, and he has been thrilled with it! For hours, he and Lani gaze at the stars in the constellations. She loves it when he makes up silly stories about how the constellations got their names. She giggles, though she also marvels at his imagination. Yes, knowing Jesse is truly an experience and a delight!

Life has been good to Jesse.

So why, at times, does he get these strange feelings? He senses that some piece to the puzzle of his life is missing. . . but which one? "Oh, well," he tells himself, "enough of this negative thinking." Tomorrow is another day, and he is looking forward to it.

Lani is, too.

This summer something exciting has happened to them. Swimming in the lagoon, they've often had the strange feeling that they weren't alone.

And then, suddenly, a huge dolphin leaps *over* them and makes a giant splash.

And *then—wait, what's that?* Jesse thinks someone is speaking to him, but there is only Lani and him and the dolphin in the water!

Could it be possible? *No, I'm just imagining it. Wow, no, I'm not!* he realizes.

The dolphin is actually communicating telepathically with him! It is so weird! The dolphin asks, "Are you my new trainers?"

I don't believe it! I actually know what he's thinking!

Yes, something unexplainable and mind-boggling is happening that afternoon. Jesse and the dolphin can read each other's minds!

Jesse wonders, *How is this possible? Do I have powers I never knew I had?*

He would have to investigate further, but he resolved to enjoy his new-found power and keep it a secret—even from Lani or, for that matter, anyone.

Again the dolphin asks, "Are you my new trainers?"

"No, we're not," Jesse replies mentally. "We're just two young people living here on this island."

"Is this part of the Ocean World Park?"

". . .No, it's not."

"Alright, then!" replies the dolphin, who has just escaped from the theme park. "I like my new freedom, and I think I'll stick around for a while."

Now, every chance they get, Jesse and Lani race to the lagoon to swim, play, and explore with their new friend. Yes, Dolphino—that's what they've named him—has become their friend. . .a new and wonderful one!

Jesse loves this time with the dolphin and especially loves talking to him about life under the surface of the water. Although they speak a different language, Lani is always amazed that Dolphino understands their every wish and command, and Jesse knows exactly what Dolphino is going to do before he actually does it.

But Jesse keeps thinking that there has to be *some* explanation for this phenomenon. Maybe it will be revealed to him soon! For now, though, it's great fun having the "big gray guy" around, and (though Jesse doesn't know it), Dolphino will not only be a great friend but also a *life saver*!

CHAPTER 2

Danny, The Wonder Dolphin

ANNY, THE WONDER DOLPHIN, was born in the Ocean World Theme Park. He had learned the art of performing at an early age. In fact, he was a ham!

He trained quickly and was the darling of the show. He loved to show off and was a natural. Although there were other dolphins in the show, Wally the whale and Sebastian the seal, Danny was the *star attraction*. People came back time and again to see him perform. He would fly around the pool with amazing speed and leap majestically into the air. For the finale, he would jump out of the water and through a series of fiery hoops! What a thrill to see him perform!

The visitors loved a hilarious routine he would do with Sebastian, the seal. Sebastian, with a whistle in his mouth, would pretend that he was Danny's trainer.

Each time the seal blew the whistle, Danny went through a short routine, and then Sebastian clapped his fins in approval. All the children, and the adults, loved it.

At the end of each show, the animals received a standing ovation! Danny's trainers loved him, too. They'd never had an animal with such a natural gift for performing.

So they were just devastated when they discovered, one evening, that he was missing!

Bill, one of the trainers, had been feeding the animals when Sue came by to chat. Because he had a crush on Sue, he got caught up in the conversation and forgot to lock the dolphin's gate. Danny, being naturally curious and inventive, quickly popped open the gate, and he swam out of his small pool of water and into a vast ocean with no boundaries and no end. It was glorious to be so free! It was *such* a marvelous feeling to swim and jump without any restrictions!

He swam lazily for miles, enjoying this newfound

freedom. When he was hungry, he had no trouble finding food. . .what a *variety*. His new surroundings were spectacular!

HE DIDN'T KNOW HOW LONG he had been swimming or how many days had elapsed since he left the Park. It didn't matter, though—he loved his new life!

One day he noticed two people swimming. He thought they must be his trainers.

Being accustomed to people, he had no fear and joined in the fun. And that's how Danny met Jesse and Lani. . .and why they would later name him "Dolphino."

CHAPTER 3

Hiring Johnson

ALTHOUGH DANNY HAD FOUND a new home and friends, the owner and staff at Ocean World were very upset! They'd lost their star performer, and besides losing a friend, they were losing business!

So the owner, John Harriman, hired a private detective, Duke Johnson, to find Danny and bring him home.

It's the most unusual case Duke has had since he started twelve years ago. He's about six feet tall and rather stocky. He always looks a little scruffy and disheveled, but he's supposed to be the best detective in the business.

This, though, is the first time his missing person is an animal named Danny the Wonder Dolphin.

He starts by driving up and down the coast, seeking any information on the sighting of a dolphin that displays any unusual qualities. For the next few weeks, he has no success at all—until, one day, he overhears two surfers, Brian and Joe, discussing a recent surfing trip south of them, not too far down the coast. They're also raving about what Brian calls "a dynamic dolphin" who was as tame as could be, and a great acrobat! No one knew where the dolphin came from, "But he was something else," Brian says, nodding enthusiastically.

That's all Duke has to hear! After getting more detailed information from the boys, he gets back in his car and drives off to see if this really could be Danny.

CHAPTER 4

The Annual Meteor Shower

THAT SATURDAY, AS THE MORNING SUN starts to creep over the mountains, Jesse has already finished his breakfast. He kisses Nanney goodbye and runs toward the cove.

Lani is already there, and so is Dolphino. The dolphin is squirting water at her, and she laughs as she dodges the spray. Jesse soon joins in the fun.

Afterward, as Lani is lying on the beach, enjoying the warmth of the sun, he gently places tiny baby crabs on her back. She jumps up screaming and laughing, then begins chasing him along the beach.

Dolphino starts squealing in delight, leaping in the

air and swimming back and forth.

They join him in the water and laugh together all afternoon.

That night, Jesse is gazing out his window, bewitched by the beautiful evening sky.

Yes, if you guessed it, you guessed right—Nanney knows the "Secret in the Sky," but she can't tell him. He might never understand! It's even harder for her to believe it all really ever happened! Perhaps she will tell him The Truth in time. . . perhaps when he's older, but not now!

Jesse is even more excited tonight, for this is the most anticipated evening of the year.

Tonight they will witness the great annual meteor shower spectacle: the famous *Night of the Shooting Stars!* Tonight, the heavens will be aglow with streaks of glorious light.

All day he has had a strange feeling that something is going to happen to him that could change his life forever! But why such a feeling? Why tonight? *Why?*

CHAPTER 5

Plethoria's Vacation Prize

WHY IS THIS EVENING SO SPECIAL? To understand Jesse's strange feelings, we must travel to a place far beyond our planet, a place like ours yet, in a way, very different.

Just beyond our Milky Way, in another galaxy, lies the planet Plethoria. Plethoria has atmospheric conditions similar to those on our own planet, and land suitable for habitation. Plethoria was formed well before our planet, though, and is consequently more technologically advanced.

It once looked as beautiful as Earth, too. But due to rapid growth and development by its inhabitants, all the lush trees, plants, flowers, and vegetation have long since been replaced by huge, formidable buildings and roadways. And, yes, it's their own fault that everything is now grown artificially inside those enormous buildings. Nothing green exists outside those complexes!

One of their outstanding technological advancements has been the development of highly refined intergalactic space travel. As a result, they staged a *very special space race.* As the highlight of the activities, contestants come to participate from every complex on the planet. Not only is the race a very exciting one, the grand prize is *spectacular!* The winner receives an *All-Expense-Paid Three-Year Vacation for Two on Planet Earth!* The winner also receives the Plethorian Medal of Excellence, the most prestigious award on the planet, which a great many contestants would risk their life for!

Planet Earth was particularly chosen for two reasons. First, because Plethorians look a lot like Earthlings, and the Plethorian lifestyle is similar to that on Earth; second, and more importantly, medal winners get a chance to see, and live on, a planet that looks like theirs did long, long ago. Lush green forests, unique plants, delicious vegetables, trees that bear delicious fruit and nuts, gorgeously scented flowers, and dense jungles are all things Plethorians had heard and read about, but that no longer existed on their planet. These wonders would be theirs to see and enjoy on their trip.

In addition, the winner of the space race has a mission: to return with seeds and samples of Earth's plant life. The winners must learn how to plant and care for these samples. The competitors are almost all young, part of a new generation of Plethorians who yearn to return their planet to its beautiful original state, to overcome the destruction caused by their ancestors concentrating so much on advance technology. These samples will enable them, they hope, to turn their barren planet into the paradise it once was.

They also need to bring back samples of Earth textiles and clothing, plus books from each location they visit, which will go to the National Museum of Plethoria, where people can study and, later, enjoy them.

THIS YEAR, CHAZ'S FATHER, SANDOR, is a contestant in the Grand Race, and Chaz is concerned—the man is no longer young and shouldn't have to risk his life. He's more important to the family than any prize trip. Chaz would like to compete, but only one family member can. And besides, his father is one of the first ever to have won the prize and the medal. Maybe that's why he's dead-set on trying again. Why else would he risk everything to win again and go back to Planet Earth?

Chaz and his friends have always talked about the time when they'd be able to enter the race. Nearly every family has, in one way or other, helped build a spacecraft for the big event. His father has worked incessantly on theirs. Chaz can't understand why his father wants to qualify as one of the finalists. "If he loses," the boy mutters as he paces back and forth in his room, "*I'll* enter and show those hotshot space heroes a thing or two!"

But for now, he knows how important the race is to his father, and he's willing to relinquish command of their ship to him.

CHAPTER 6

Mother's Story

CHAZ THINKS, *It's all about tomorrow. Father has finally qualified for the race. In fact, he's at the launch site checking out last-minute details.*

The boy knows that the race will be difficult, dangerous, and at the same time *thrilling.* Not only will he have to make it to the finish line first, but he will also have to dodge, or disintegrate, the streams of the oncoming asteroids as they shower down around him.

And there have been many times when a contestant didn't even make it home! And—

"Stop!" he practically shouts. "I don't even want to think like that!"

"Chaz, Chaz!" he hears his mother Astrid calling. It startles him. Her voice sounds very strange, and he can tell she's worried.

She finds him in his room. "Son," she tells him, "your father is very ill. He just called. He'll. . .he'll *never* be able to compete in the race. What are we going to do? It may be our last opportunity!" She breaks into tears.

Chaz races to the arena, where he's shocked to find his father utterly distraught. He never noticed how tired, how much older, he'd become in a few short years. The strain and emotional cost of preparing for the race has certainly taken a toll on his health. Chaz knows that, if Father goes in this condition, he'll never make it back!

"Come on, Father, you need to get some rest," he says, and puts his arm around the older man. "Let's get you home."

But on the way back, he hears him mumble over and over, "I *have* to race! I *have* to race! I need to *win* to get back to planet Earth!"

"*What?* You—you *can't* go!" Chaz tells him. "You have a fever. You're burning up, Father! And you don't *need* to win!"

"All right. Maybe a short rest will do me some good."

When they get home, Chaz helps him lie down in the bedroom, turns out the light, closes the door, and finds his mother in the kitchen.

She meets his eyes and shrugs. Chaz takes a seat and asks, "Why's Father so upset? Is there something I should know? He can't fly. He's too sick!"

Astrid sits across from him at the little wooden table where they have always shared their meals. She lays a hand on his and sighs. "Chaz, no else can hear what I am about to tell you, no one, until the matter is resolved," she says in a trembling voice.

". . .I understand, Mother. I won't say a word to anybody. Now *please* tell me what this *obsession* is that you and Father have about this race and the trip to Earth."

She sips tea, nods, sighs again, and whispers, "As you know, many years ago Father won the race, and the trip. Oh, what a wonderful *adventure* it was going to be! It was *so* exciting to be part of the project to bring back those precious samples everybody was waiting for. And we could choose any destination we wanted on Earth, and it was going to be for *three years!*"

Her voice grew huskier, and she seemed to be gazing into a far-distant thought. "Well, some, you know, choose the jungle, the rain forest, desert regions, colder landforms, or anywhere else on the planet. We both chose to land in a place called 'Hawaii.' We flew to Earth, as each previous winner had done, during its annual meteor shower, or, as they call it, *The Night of the Shooting Stars.*

"People there exclaimed, 'Look at *that* star! It's so beautiful!' Little did they know that it was *our* spaceship traveling undetected through Earth's atmosphere!

CHAPTER 7

Earth

A STRID CONTINUES, "THE FIRST GLIMPSE of our new home was breathtaking, Chaz. We could not get over how beautiful the blue-green water was. What a truly magnificent sight—lush green trees, bright flowers everywhere, and that gorgeous, majestic landscape! You can't imagine—no one could ever imagine—what we've given up for technology! There'd be so much to show, to tell our friends about, when we returned. And we hoped and prayed that the Earth people we met would be equally as beautiful, and equally as welcoming.

"After we landed behind a huge rocky outcrop, we

beamed our ship back to Plethoria, programmed to return exactly three years later. We had, you know, mimicked their monetary system, so that we would have enough of the Earth's exchange paper to live comfortably. We needed to find suitable lodging somewhere along that beautiful beach.

"So we asked around in a town nearby, and we learned from a sweet old fellow that a very charming lady named Nanney had a lovely guest house right on the beach and was looking for renters.

"'What luck,' we thought. And when we met her, we discovered she was everything he'd said—happy-go-lucky, caring, a person easy to become friendly with. . .and she did become a very dear friend. . . ."

Astrid shakes her head and again looks deeply into her son's eyes. "Yet it was because of this friendship and trust that our vacation was both memorable and tragic! Life there was such a joy! Father soon began to go out with the fishermen, and I learned the ways of the Earth women from Nanney.

"Just before we left for Earth, I learned that I was *pregnant*. We were just so thrilled. And it would be the first Plethorian child to ever be born on Earth. As my pregnancy was drawing to a close, Nanney became as excited as we were. She'd never had a child of her own, you see. . . . Well, when I went into labor, something extraordinary happened—instead of *one* child being born, there were *two*.

"*Two!* I had given birth to *twin boys!* Never before had a Plethorian given birth to twins!

"You were beautiful, healthy boys, and you and your brother—we named him Jesse—flourished in that magnificent setting," Astrid continued in a voice that had grown somewhat shaky.

"And then. . .and then, as time passed, we had to make plans to return here, to our real home. We told Nanney that we would soon have to leave. As you can guess, she was heartbroken."

Chaz clasped his hands together. "I knew I'd been born on Earth, but—well, this is totally unexpected. I never knew I had a *twin brother!*" he exclaimed in disbelief. "Did he die on Earth? How awful, how sad, to win such a wonderful trip only to lose a child!"

"No, my son," she said tearfully. "Jesse must still be

alive on Earth. *This* has been our heart-wrenching secret!"

". . .Huh? I-I don't understand."

Astrid laid her hands on his. "Let me explain. Nanney had somehow learned who we actually were, I don't know how but she's very intuitive, and she also later overheard your father discussing our departure plans, when and where the spacecraft would land. She confronted us, and we just *had* to tell her our secret. She loved us so much, and, most especially, you boys.

"Well, she swore never to reveal our secret. As a token of our love and appreciation, I gave her the ring that the women in my family have passed down from mother to daughter for generations. It was beautiful, with a very unusual purple stone. I decided that, if anyone asked about the ring, I'd tell them I lost it while I was swimming. . . .

"And then, on the day of our departure, something *terrible* happened! When we set out to gather you both, it was as if your brother had *vanished*. We searched everywhere. Our spacecraft arrived, and we were frantic! The ship's engines were turned on automatically from back home. We had to board immediately! *And no one was allowed to remain on Earth!* We—we had to come up with some plan. And then it came to us! They would never have to know that *two boys* had been born. Twins had never been born on Plethoria. So our secret would be safe!"

She sighed and touched his hand. "So we gathered our samples and boarded that ship with just *you!* Jesse remained on Earth. . .and so did a piece of our hearts!"

She was sobbing by then. "We were devastated, but there was nothing we could do, and we couldn't even tell a soul!"

"Could he have survived on Earth all this time?" asked Chaz.

"Yes," she said. "Because he was born there, he would eventually become adjusted to that environment. And I know that Nanney searched for Jesse but couldn't find him either. She only discovered the next day that Christie, one of our neighbors, had taken him, thinking it was her afternoon to babysit. What a tragic misunderstanding! We didn't know that then. We're pretty sure of it now.

"As we departed, your father swore he wouldn't rest until he'd won another Grand Meteor Race that would enable us to return to Earth and bring our son home."

FROM THE MOMENT ASTRID AND SANDOR LEFT that day, Nanney had realized that she was responsible for little Jesse. She could only honor his parents by both loving and protecting their precious child.

Now Chaz knows what he has to do. He will have to take his sick father's place in the race. Fortunately, he has helped his father and is able to fly the ship, thanks to his training at the Acedemy.

It will not be an easy race but such an important one. Finally, he understands!

CHAPTER 8

The Race

IT'S JUST ABOUT TIME for the finalists to board their spacecraft. Sandor is too weak to come to the blast-off station, but Astrid is there. No one recognizes Chaz in his father's spacesuit, especially with the gold shield and white helmet covering his face.

He waves to the other contestants, and they wave back. Before he boards the ship, Astrid gives him a kiss and points to the family pendant he is wearing on the necklace around his neck. She says it will keep him safe and remind him of their love. It will also help him identify his brother, because Jesse was wearing the same Necklace and Pendant when they left. As he enters the ship, Chaz feels an uncanny sensation of exhilaration. This will be the challenge of his life!

There are twenty-five qualifiers in the race, all eager to win the prize and the medal! For a moment, he sits motionless, looking at the control panel. Will he remember all that they taught him at the Academy? It was fun racing against his friends, but now it will be a matter of survival—*his* survival! He remembers that over three hundred pilots tried out, and only twenty-five were selected. This year his father qualified, and they were so proud of him. Now, Chaz has to use all his own skills and expertise to win!

The referee is soon waving the contestants to the starting line with his bright-purple flag. *Oh, no!* Chaz has to be sandwiched in between Maurado on his right and Zerrod (they call him "Zee") on his left, two of Plethoria's best pilots! Maurado is the most daring, and he has an attitude that makes him intimidating as well as obnoxious. To know him is to fear him! When you meet him, his piercing eyes seem to sear right through your body. He's a frightening figure in that black-and-silver, sinister-looking spacecraft and suit. . .and, boy, will he be a dangerous opponent!

Turning to his left, Chaz can see Zee. He's different. Although an outstanding pilot, he isn't devious but a very friendly, outgoing person. Zee waves, and Chaz, knowing his gold-colored shield is covering his face and identity, waves back.

Having failed to win the race in the last few years, Zee is certain that this is his year. He says out loud, "Chaz's father will be no competition, but Maurado is another story—he's trouble. He's a fantastic pilot but also a genuine scoundrel who can't be trusted!"

As Maurado taxies his ship to the starting line, his sinister eyes scan the other crafts. He sees Zee is there and tells himself, *The others won't pose much of a threat, but I'll make sure he doesn't either! It will be all mine. . .not only the prize, but, more importantly, the Medal of Excellence!*

All Chaz can see and hear are the throngs of people screaming and cheering the pilots on with words of encouragement.

Then the purple flag comes down once, and all the engines roar to life. For a moment, the crowd is silent, and a voice comes through a loudspeaker counting down to zero: *10, 9, 8, 7*—Chaz takes a deep breath, and his fingers begin to fly over the keyboard—*6, 5, 4, 3, 2, 1. . .* *Blast-Off!* He hits the ignition release, and his ship explodes into the sky. What a *feeling!* His takeoff is perfect, and the race has begun!

Flying at supersonic speed is fantastic, but dangerous! It's even more thrilling than Chaz has ever imagined. Reading about it at the academy is one thing. Experiencing it is something *else!*

Still, though soaring through the heavens is exciting, that's *not* what the race is all about.

In a flash, he passes one ship, then three, then five. He is off to a great start! With asteroids whizzing by his ship, Chaz aims his laser-blaster gun carefully. He knows that he will have only one opportunity to disintegrate an oncoming asteroid before it smashes into his ship and destroys, not only his father's hopes, but his as well! It's difficult, frightening, and exhilarating—but if he makes even one small mistake, he tells himself, all will be lost!

"No," he mutters to himself, nervously touching his control panel, as other ships and very large chunks of rock hurtle by, "I can't lose, I can't! It means so much to Mother and Father. . .*and now to me!*"

With not a moment to waste, he squeezes the trigger on his weapon and fires at a huge asteroid coming straight at him, screaming, "There, take *that*, you hunk of space junk, you no-good-piece-of-rock!"

Then he hears a series of abrasive clicks and pulls up and out of the way in a long arc that quickly bends back on itself. "No, no!" he shouts frantically, eyes on a blinking red light on the left of his dashboard. "My laser blaster is jammed. I gotta get it *working*. My life depends on this weapon!"

He tries not to panic, keenly attuned to the seriousness of the situation. Maybe the trigger got loose, or maybe the adapter coil's stuck? Using one hand to steer the ship, he reaches into the console with the other to identify it. He slams the joystick to the right, barely avoiding another asteroid, eyes straight ahead of him. "That's it!" he exclaims. That's *it!* It's the adapter coil, and I gotta reconnect it—wait, what's that. . .*another* asteroid? Come on! Come *on*. Stretch, stretch, *stretch*, you coil!" he shouts. He's careening through space without an active weapon, cutting the ship back and forth as sweat pours down his forehead and he can hardly see.

"Yes! I've hooked it back!" he screams triumphantly. "Now, fire, fire, fire! Yes, it works! Great shot, great shot! Now, let's put this ship into supersonic speed and get away from these flying hunks of rock!"

But just as Chaz is telling himself that he's going to win the race, two ships tear right past him!

"Oh, no—it's Zee and Maurado!"

As they zoom past the old man's ship, they are both astounded. What's *with this old man?* they both wonder. He couldn't be this daring, and *never* this fast! *What's going on?* Both had always written him off; he had never posed a real threat. Now, he's become a *problem* to be reckoned with. They'll have to keep an eye on him if he ever catches up with them—which, they tell themselves, is not very likely.

The pitch-darkness of space, and the luminous stars, provide a magnificent backdrop for the race.

Zee and Maurado are now alone on the course, but, just to be certain, Maurado checks his radar scope.

Now! Now's the right time, thinks Maurado. *I'll let him pass me and wait for the next asteroid, and then. . . .*

As soon as another asteroid plummets toward their ships, Maurado engages his laser blaster and takes careful aim. He will make it look like an accident. He fires. The invisible beam plows into the rock! To avoid being hit, he immediately veers to the right. He can see rock fragments hammering against Zee's ship, just as he planned. A huge piece slams into his ventilator, causing a tremendous explosion!

Zee's ship shakes violently. Losing speed, Zee tries to regain control, but, realizing he can't finish the race, he sends out a distress signal, hoping that he will be rescued.

Maurado smirks and thinks, *Poor Zee. What a pity, what a shame!* When he returns home, he will be so *devastated* when he hears of Zee's tragedy.

But at that instant, Chaz streaks past him. "What? I can't believe it!" Maurado screams. "It's that old man's ship again! He's passing me, and I—I can't do a thing to stop him! How could he catch up with me so fast? It's too late! It's too late! He's going to win!"

With the race almost over, Chaz keeps gaining on

Maurado as they hurtle toward his final destination. But *no!* There's one last asteroid heading right for his ship, one last obstacle to overcome! His hand begins to shake, but he stills it by sheer force of will, aims as if he has hours to instead of seconds, and fires. Yes—a direct hit! *The race is his! He has won!* At last, he will be given the chance to *find his brother and bring him home!*

After all the ships have landed and the pilots have begun to disembark, Chaz descends the steps to thunderous applause and cheering. He spots Zee, who made it back, and waves. But when he takes off his helmet, he is stunned by the sudden silence of the crowd.

Immediately, Plethorian guards surround him and they drag him to the Great One's viewing box—because he's not a qualified contestant. He is in trouble!

Under heated questioning, Chaz nods and raises his hand. Silence descends on those in the box. "My father became very seriously ill at the last moment," he says. "He could barely stand up straight. He couldn't fly, so I took his place.

BECAUSE OF THE GRAVITY of this unprecedented situation,

the Great One calls an emergency meeting of the Grand Council. That night Chaz and his family are summoned to appear before it. In fact, the entire community arrives that evening to see how the matter will be resolved.

Maurado is wondering the same thing, but for a different reason. Perhaps he hasn't lost after all! If the Council disqualifies Chaz, *he* will be the Grand Prize Winner!

CHAPTER 9

The Grand Council

THE PLETHORIAN PROSECUTOR RISES from his seat, rearranges the heavy cloak on his shoulders, clears his throat, and declares in a deep voice, "Great One, members of the Grand Council, and citizens, we have before us an issue of the gravest concern! An issue of legitimacy is surrounding the outcome of our principal space competition. This boy who comes before us, as no doubt you have all heard, won this year's competition. But," he goes on, raising his arm and pointing a long finger at Chaz, "he is *not* a legitimate qualifier. Consequently, he is not, cannot be, a legitimate winner! He has his reasons, to be sure. But no reason, it is my duty to point out, could sufficiently excuse that fundamental disqualification."

He resumes his seat. The immediate silence that falls is like a sudden weight on those gathered in the high-ceilinged chamber. The bailiff, an older gentleman with graying hair, calls out, "The defendant will rise."

Chaz gets to his feet.

The Great One slowly turns to face him. "What do you have to say in your defense, young man?" he asks. "Your father could very well have disqualified himself and entered the race again at some future time."

"May it please you, Great One," says Chaz, "I know it was a serious breach of the rules, but it was imperative that I win this year," he says in a voice that adroitly combined humility with strength. He pauses, still uncertain of how to proceed. If he tells them the truth, he will reveal his family secret, and he promised his mother he would never do that. He glances at his mother and father for some sign.

Sensing his son's distress, Sandor hauls himself to his feet. "Great One, may I address the Council?"

A long pause follows, at the end of which the Great

One nods in assent. "You may."

His father clears his throat and slowly unravels the story—and their long-kept secret of the twins. "When it was time for my wife to give birth, instead of just one child born, there were twin boys. Then, as it was time to leave, my other son was nowhere to be found, and we had no choice but to leave him behind! Chaz desperately wanted to win this race and be able to bring my other son home."

Astrid, who has been sitting quietly beside him, nods painfully as he goes on, tears streaming down her cheeks.

The Council, and the visitors packing the chamber, are speechless, and some are shedding tears, too.

Then the Great One and the Council retire to the inner chamber to discuss, and eventually rule on, the matter.

Those in the great chamber await their return and their verdict as the light pouring in through the tall, narrow windows softens with the passage of the light.

Hours later, the Great One and his council re-enter, looking stern, and all wonder: *What will their decision be?* Whispered conversations immediately end, and the silence stretches out as the judicial panel members settle themselves in their seats.

The bailiff calls out, "The defendant will rise."

Chaz takes a deep breath and does so.

The Great One meets the young man's eyes and, for a moment, stares deeply into them. "The Council and I have decided that, because of the circumstances—the very *unusual* circumstances—surrounding this matter, and the fact that *no one* from our planet must ever remain on Earth, we will award you and your family the Grand Prize.

"But *not* the Medal of Excellence. That we will withhold. Your mission will be to find your brother you call Jesse and *bring him home*. This matter now rests," he concludes, and, as he and the council depart, the entire gathering explodes in an uproar of cheering as Chaz's mother and father embrace, waving and calling out "Thank you, thank you!"

When he heard the verdict, Zee was thrilled for his friend, but Maurado shrieked, "*WHAT?*" Unable to believe what he was hearing, he kicked over one of the tables in his fury, screaming, "Everything that I risked to win has been for *nothing*. It's all been taken *away* from me by a—a boy. . .a *nobody!*" He storms out of the room, shaking his fist and promising that Chaz and his family will pay dearly for what they've done to him!

Chaz knows what he has to do. He begins preparing himself and his ship for the trip. Wanting to remain undetected, he will be beamed down to Earth during the annual *Night of the Shooting Stars* meteor shower. It will look as if his ship is just another "shooting star." He asked to land in a place called "Hawaii," at the same coordinates that his mother and father chose so long ago.

It won't be a vacation trip for him, though, but a quest to find his missing brother. Will he recognize him? Will the necklace be helpful? And how will Jesse react when he finds out *the truth? Can I somehow convince him to return home with me,* Chaz asks himself, *where he belongs?*

All these questions will soon be answered.

CHAPTER 10

The Night Of The Shooting Stars

WHAT A CELEBRATION THEY HAVE that night! Jesse, Lani and Nanney have an absolute feast of a dinner! Afterwards, they go to their favorite hilltop to witness the meteor shower they call "The Night of the Shooting Stars."

Wow! This year's is *especially* spectacular! The sky is aglow with streaks of light. One in particular *outshines* all others. Jesse can't help but feel there is something very *special* about it! Its strange beauty touches him. He is mesmerized. What is it? Why does *this* shooting star seem so different? Why these strange feelings? Why *this* evening?

Chaz's ship has shot right through the atmosphere, looking, as he hoped, just like any other shooting star. When he lands, his spacecraft is immediately beamed back home. He sets out on foot to find the town where the adventure began.

He tramps along for days through lush mountainous terrain covered with tall, massive trees and dense undergrowth. He's struck by flowers of every hue glittering in the mist, and by the variety of luscious scents.

When he enters the first town he finds, he is astonished by the simplicity of their civilization. The houses are small and simple, the transportation crude. The Earthlings have such a long way to go to in order to compete with his planet.

Acting like a surfer bum, he can easily move around without drawing suspicion as he searches for this woman named Nanney. She will, if all goes well, lead him to his brother—who, *hopefully*, will be wearing the necklace.

Thus begins his search from city to city and from town to town.

Earth is such a beautiful planet. Surfing was fun, but

not half as much fun as flying your own spaceship! He is
not on vacation, though, but on a mission—a very, very
important one!

~

CHAPTER 11

Finding Jesse

J ESSE HAS HIS OWN WAY of surfing. Island people call him the "Dolphin Boy" because he holds onto Dolphino's fin and rides the crest of the waves. It's thrilling to see them skimming over, and through, the water. What a sight!

That's how Chaz first hears of the famous duo. He's sitting under a big, colorful umbrella at a lunch place by the beach, listening to the waves crash on the sand and watching young people ride the big waves. As he munches on a delicious bowl of poke, he catches part of a conversation between two locals at the counter.

"Yes, sir," says a woman in a loose flowery dress, who

has just swallowed a bite of a cheeseburger, "that's what I hear. Kid actually swims with that fish. People've seen it."

"First of all, Mary Lou," says the guy sitting next to her in a floral shirt and a pair of faded shorts, "that's not a *fish*. It's a *dolphin*, see?"

"A dolphin, then. What difference does it make, Joe? Kid swims with it, they say."

"Where?" Joe asks, and takes a sip of the iced tea he's having to wash down his fish taco.

She waves her hand up the beach. "I don't know. Up there somewhere, they say."

Chaz squints at the two. Something has drawn him to this conversation and sparked his intuition. He wants to see for himself.

It starts him on a quest that seems to take forever. He discovers that quite a few people have heard the story of a boy swimming with a big dolphin. But Hawaii is a big island, and there are also many beaches. Maybe this is the one he has been looking for. Chad decides to check this one out.

He hits this beach and starts to ask around.

"You want to know about the Dolphin Boy?" asks Grace.

"I sure do—I want to see them with my own two eyes."

"Well," she says, grinning, "then you have come to the right place, friend!" She points to the water.

Chaz turns—*and there they are:* a boy gliding through the surf next to a magnificent dolphin.

When the boy finally swims ashore and rises out of the water, Chaz cannot believe his eyes. There, around his neck, hangs *the necklace with the pendant!* What a *miracle!*

It *is* his brother. . .*Jesse!* If Mother and Father could see him now, they would be so proud.

Slowly, he approaches. "Hi," he says. "That's really something, what you do."

"Thanks."

"How long have you been swimming with him? He *is* a him, right?"

Jesse grins at that, and his teeth, almost blindingly white in his tanned face, glitter. "Yeah, he is. We call him Dolphino. I think it's been a while now."

"Wow! That must be awesome."

"I'll say."

The bond between the boys is immediate, and they quickly become friends. Jesse is drawn to the stranger who, for some reason, reminds him of himself. He's tall and well-built too, but he has dark, shoulder-length hair tied in the back.

Jesse holds out a fist. "I'm Jesse, by the way."

Chaz taps it with his own. "They call me Chaz."

RIGHT FROM THE BEGINNING, Jesse finds his new friend extremely fascinating. In the days to come, so does Lani. Later in the week, Jesse invites him to dinner to meet his mother. "You'll like her," he says. She's really cool. Her name's Nanney.

Could she be the same Nanney who started it all? Chaz wonders.

When he meets her, he instantly realizes she hasn't got a mean bone in her body. And when he sees the way she looks at Jesse and speaks to him, he can tell that she truly loves him. He glances at her hands, and there's his mother's ring! That confirms it!

For the next few weeks, Jesse, Lani, and Chaz will spend many days and evenings eating at Nanney's while talking, laughing, and surfing. The three young people and Dolphino grow inseparable.

CHAPTER 12

The Necklace and Pendant

BUT THE DETECTIVE, DUKE JOHNSON—remember him?—has also heard of a "Dolphin Boy" surfing with a magnificently talented dolphin. Duke knows that Danny, a real ham who loves performing, is one of the most intelligent dolphins ever to perform in a water show. The detective has figured the odds are pretty good that it is "the" Danny he has been searching for, and decides to see for himself.

It's taken him even longer to track down the right beach than it took Chaz, but when he finally lays his eyes on the spectacular duo skimming over the water, he has no doubt at all. He's certain that magnificent dolphin *is*

Danny!

He also notices something else—a beautiful necklace with an unusual center stone on the boy's pendant. He can tell it's a valuable piece, and he *has* to have it—as well as the dolphin!

As Johnson sits on the beach, trying to come up with a plan, he spots Jesse surfing and playing around with the creature. They're having such a good time that Jesse is unaware of a huge wave barreling in from the distance.

The wave upends him and knocks him off the board with tremendous force. He spins furiously in the foaming water. Johnson watches this with amusement, waiting to see what will happen next.

But he never once takes his eyes off the necklace gleaming in the bright sunlight.

And then he sees Jesse's necklace fly off his neck. His eyes are riveted to the necklace, following its every movement. Not even removing his shoes, he races through the surf to the spot where it has landed. Groping furiously in the sand, he is finally rewarded. He can't quite see it yet, but he knows he has it in his hand. He stuffs it in his pocket, sand and all.

As soon as he gets back to his hotel room, he shuts the door, pulls the necklace out of his pocket, and realizes it is *magnificent!* In the center of the pendant sits the most exquisite, uniquely colored stone he has ever seen. He *must* have it examined and appraised by an expert!

The next day he makes an appointment to see Harry Miller, a jeweler and gemologist he's known for years, on another part of the island.

When he shows him the necklace, Miller is astonished. Never in his life has he seen such unusual metal or such a perfect stone. It is flawless! "Where did you get this from, Duke?" he asks excitedly. "Who owns it? This is an *extremely valuable* piece of jewelry!" More astounding still, the materials they're made of *are not* found on this planet!

Johnson can't believe it! He now knows that he has stumbled upon something more valuable than Danny the Wonder Dolphin.

His adrenaline skyrockets! He tells Harry there will be a hefty profit in it for him if he keeps his mouth shut. After photographing the necklace for security purposes, Harry agrees.

Now that Johnson has the necklace, he has to have the *boy, too!* he tells himself on his drive back to the beach. Just think what a government would pay to have an "actual" alien in its midst! Besides, where there is one gem, or one alien, there must be more. Who knows what riches are to be discovered!

"Rich. . . . *Rich!*" He will become rich and famous! The boy and the necklace are his ticket to both.

He begins to formulate a plan to *kidnap* Jesse. He will enlist his heavily built, kooky friend Mack, who lives not far away, to help him do it.

When Johnson meets Mack, he tells him the boy's father is worth millions, and that they will split the ransom money.

Mack is so gullible, he believes this story completely—and definitely wants to take part in the kidnapping!

CHAPTER 13

The Kidnapping

OVER THE NEXT FEW DAYS, Johnson monitors Lani, Jesse, and Chaz's every move from a hidden spot in a grove of palms. He notices that Jesse and Chaz will surf at sunset while Lani builds a campfire and cooks dinner.

That Wednesday evening, he decides to set his plan with Mack in motion. They aren't disappointed. In fact, they're relieved to see that Chaz isn't with the other two, who are on the stretch of beach by themselves.

After surfing, Jesse joins her for dinner by the campfire.

Mack and Johnson stroll casually down the beach toward them and engage in polite conversation. They recognize Mack and Johnson as the gentlemen who have also been regularly watching the surfers. Johnson tells them he is looking for contestants for the surfing contest everyone is talking about, which will soon be held in Australia. "I'm one of the promoters," he tells Jesse. "I've been looking at the talent all over this island, and I must say I'm most impressed with you. How would you like to represent your island in the contest?"

Jesse is thrilled, and honored to be considered. "Why, sure!" he says, nodding enthusiastically.

Mack, who has been drifting to the left, suddenly grabs Lani. Startled, she shrieks and tries to shake him off, but he's much too strong for her. Jesse throws himself at the assailant, but he's too late—Johnson has shifted his weight forward and punches him hard in the stomach, knocking the breath out of him and, while Jesse is dazed, throws a strong arm around the boy's neck and starts dragging him to their boat.

But the boy begins to struggle and kick.

Johnson grumbles, "Some help you are, Mack! All you have to do is tie up a little girl, leave her on the beach, and get the boat started. If you don't do something fast, this kid will get away—and so will all our money!

Mack sees that Johnson is having trouble handling the boy. He races over to the struggling pair, grabs the paddle, and slams it against Jesse's head. That stuns him, and Mack quickly ties his hands and throws him in the boat. The necklace and pendant are valuable, Johnson knows, but the kid is the key to the mystery and could be even more valuable than *any* piece of jewelry!

JESSE SLOWLY REGAINS CONSCIOUSNESS. For a moment, he can't remember what has happened. All he can hear is Johnson's coarse voice. And then, as his vision clears, he can't believe what he is seeing. . .*Johnson is wearing his necklace!*

He thinks, "What is this guy doing with it? Who *are* these two? Why would they want to kidnap *me?* Is he really a promoter? Why did he make up that surfing story? Why are they *doing* this?"

He knows, though, that he has no time to lose. He has to get out of this dilemma as soon as possible. He hopes he can still swim to the shore from this distance, but if he waits any longer, it will be too late. He prays for guidance. Between the distance and the darkness, he will never see his home or his loved ones again. Terrified, he knows he must do something. . . and do it quickly!

He notices a small gas can next to his feet. Because Mack was in a hurry when he tied the boy's wrists, he did a sloppy job. This enables Jesse to undo the rope, free his hands and, seizing the can, slams it against Mack's head. Then he throws it at Johnson, momentarily stunning him. He yanks the necklace off Johnson's neck and dives into the water.

The water and the darkness engulf him. If only he had his surfboard with him, it would be easier. Then something brushes against him. Could it—could it be that his prayers have been answered by none other than *Dolphino?* Yes. . .it *is* Dolphino, his loyal friend! Realizing Jesse is in danger, he has swum toward Johnson's boat. Instinctively, he knows that he has to rescue his friend from these men. With all his speed, he rams the boat so hard that the two men fall overboard into the dark, menacing water.

The boy grabs Dolphino's fin, and Jesse's dear friend

brings him to safety. He hugs Dolphino as he expresses his heartfelt gratitude. Dolphino then squeals his love for Jesse while spinning around.

Nobody knows what happens to Johnson and Mack that night, for the next day only the wreckage of their boat washes ashore.

CHAPTER 14

The Moment Of Reckoning

On Wednesday evening, Chaz is supposed to join Jesse and Lani for dinner at the beach, but he is delayed. Suddenly, a strange feeling comes over him. Something isn't right, *and it has to do with his brother*. He just knows it! But *what*?

He races to the beach. Just as it comes into view, he sees something that strikes fear into his heart—his brother being dragged by two men onto a boat and taken out to sea. What happens next he will never forget! He sees and hears those men struggling in the water, and then, out of the ocean darkness, his brother is clutching Dolphino's fin swimming towards the shore, looking distraught!

Chaz senses that Jesse has been in some sort of danger but is safe. What a relief! *What would I have told my parents,* he wonders—*that I found my brother only to lose him! They would never understand. Who were those men? Why would they be after Jesse? Do they. . .do they know the* secret? *If they did, how did they find out?*

He sees Jesse racing through the surf onto the beach, desperately searching for something—or *some-one.* At that moment, he realizes that Lani is missing. It has to be her there! He races towards them.

Jesse quickly discovers Lani. Thank goodness, she is safe and unharmed. He unties her, and they embrace. Just then, Chaz joins them.

Lani is sobbing hysterically and very upset. They finally calm her down. She wants to know why the men attacked them. He tells her that they must be crooks, because all they are interested in is his necklace.

As they make their way to the police station, Jesse nervously repeats how grateful he is to be safe and to know that she is, too. But he also wonders what those men really wanted from him. . .was it *just* the necklace?

AFTER REPORTING THE INCIDENT to the police, the boys bring Lani home and then head back to Nanney's. As they sink onto the old rattan armchairs on the porch, Jesse looks at Chaz as if he is seeing him for the very first time. All of a sudden, he realizes how much alike they are. He also feels a strong bond between them, a bond somehow greater than that between friends.

Chaz nods, having read his brother's mind, and asks him to put out his hand. When Jesse does, Chaz places his own *necklace* into it!

Jesse cannot believe what he's seeing—it's like his *own necklace*, but it has come from Chaz's pocket!

Yes! It is the *necklace* that Johnson was after. It must be very valuable! Johnson must want to know where it came from, and how he had come to own it. Jesse knows very little about its history—only that it belonged to his father and mother.

How in the world does this boy have the same necklace?

CHAPTER 15

The Truth

THAT NIGHT IS THE *RIGHT TIME*—the time for Chaz to tell Jesse why he has come, who he is, and what must be done. They are sitting on the porch, and Chaz very slowly unravels their parents' story. It is the most *astounding* story Jesse has ever heard, and can't believe he is actually a part of it. . .the story of a world beyond our Milky Way, of a land far away from planet Earth. He hears how he disappeared just as they were going away, and why they had to leave him behind. He is stunned by what he hears, is speechless, and just stares at Chaz.

He hears how heartbroken his mother and father had been on that spacecraft, how they'd had no other choice with everything on a tight schedule and no room for delay, to leave Jesse behind.

Chaz tells him how his father entered the race, hoping to win another trip to Earth to search for their lost son, and how, this year, he fell so ill he couldn't fly or compete, and how Chaz took his place and actually won.

When his brother has finished, a long silence descends on the two brothers. Jesse is in shock but knows in his heart and mind that he has just heard the *truth*.

"Tell me about them," he finally says, "about my mother and father, what their names are, do I have any *other* brothers or sisters? And—and describe Plethoria. How do people live there? How do they travel? You must be so advanced for you to be able to come here. It must be. . .spectacular!" He looks Chaz in the eyes and adds, "I always *knew* that there was something more to my life that I couldn't comprehend!"

Jesse is so curious and excited that they talk all night.

THE NEXT MORNING, WHEN JESSE and Chaz enter the house, Nanney is having her breakfast.

As they approach, she notices Jesse looks different.

At that moment, he asks her to put out her hand. He places the two necklaces in it. Realizing that *Chaz is really Jesse's twin brother*, and that he finally knows the truth, she catches her breath, and tears begin to stream down her face.

No longer holding in the secret that has tormented her all these years, she begins to tell the whole story.

"When it was time for you to leave, I didn't think to check with Christie, the babysitter, to see if you were with her," she tells Jesse. "We—we all panicked, but there was no time to search for you. No time! And we knew your parents, and your brother, had no choice but to leave without you. The spaceship wouldn't—couldn't—wait!"

Silence descends. She finally draws a breath and asks him, "What will you do? Return with your brother? Or stay here with me, Lani, and Dolphino? Whatever you decide to do, my dear boy, I will accept."

Although he loves Nanney, Dolphino, and Lani, he has always known in his heart that he is different. He never understood why until last night. He doesn't belong here. The call of the heavens is too strong for him to re-sist—"something" far beyond, always seemed to beckon him. That's where he belongs! To go with Chaz is the right decision, but it is a sad one, too. He knows he will always love Nanney, always think of her as a mother, but his place must be with his true family *in a new world.*

The next day, Chaz and Jesse begin to make plans for their return home during the next meteor shower.

FINALLY, THAT DAY AT LONG LAST ARRIVES, and Plethoria has sent them their returning spacecraft. The time has come!

That night, just as they have done in the past years, Nanney and Lani go to their favorite hilltop spot to watch the annual meteor shower—except this time Jesse isn't with them. Nanney tells the girl that he and Chaz have left for Australia as part of that international surfing team. Soon, she will tell her the truth too—she knows that Lani will keep their secret.

That night, *the Night of the Shooting Stars*, Lani notices an unusually bright glow in the heavens, but, oddly enough, instead of this star falling down towards Earth, this one is shooting *straight up!* It speeds upward and into the beyond! Nanney notices it, too. But *she* knows it's Jesse and Chaz. . .finally returning home!

As she touches her ring, she wonders if she will ever see them again. She hopes that perhaps, someday, the boys will return—at least to visit.

Perhaps. . .

perhaps. . .

perhaps. . .!

CHAPTER 16

Bad News from Plethoria

A S THEY WERE PREPARING TO TAKE OFF, Jesse didn't want to worry Nanney, but Chaz had received a message from their father that terrible things were happening on Plethoria.

Murado and his followers had taken control of the planet and imprisoned The Great One, the entire Council, and anyone who tried to challenge him. Mother, Father and Zee managed to escape into the mountains with a group of their friends.

And that was not all! Murado's evil group has built a monstrous spaceship called the DragoX2, which has a huge, magnet-like attachment capable of exuding a weird green mist that will encircle and suck up people *on any planet*—to become slaves on Plethoria!

Murado has in this way successfully captured all the beings on the planet Gorgo and enslaved them in the mines. Just imagine how horrible that must have been! These beings working in the fields, children studying in the academies, mothers feeding their babies, all suddenly heard this roaring and felt a strange force coming over them. They disappeared into that weird green mist, through the atmosphere, and into the dreadful Metal Monster.

Murado's next target, Chaz learned to his horror, was the remaining people on Plethoria! *He's bent on his revenge,* Sandor told his son. *He doesn't know you are returning with Jesse.*

There may be a way to stop this treacherous villain. But to do it, you will have to destroy that monstrous craft with Murado in it! We're hoping that you and your brother can somehow achieve this—because all of us have tried and failed.

At that moment, Chaz remembers a story told he heard as a little boy about a *"Special Ship,"* encased in the side of a mountain, that could destroy any other craft in the universe. Many had attempted to activate it, but none had been able to. But legend had it that the ship would be activated in a "very special and unique way" by those worthy to do so, and that, once activated, it would take *three* to navigate it.

Jesse and Chaz hope with all their hearts that they will figure out the secret, destroy Murado, and, in turn, save Nanney, Lani, and the rest of the planets.

But they need *three* to navigate the fabled ship. If all of Plethoria's people have tried and failed, who can they get?

BEFORE THEY LEAVE, JESSE KNOWS he will have to tell Dolphino that he is leaving. He finds him swimming in the lagoon. After Jesse relates the entire story, and his dilemma, Dolphino leaps into the air and tells him not to worry—he has *a solution! Yes! He* will be the third pilot—like Jesse, with some instruction from Chaz, he'll easily figure out how to navigate that craft.

But to take this mammal with them, Chaz has to devise an aquatic, hydro-oxygenated tank that continuously recycles the elements to make breathable oxygen for Dolphino plus dehydrated fish for his food. Chaz knows that, once they reach their planet, because of their advanced technology, Dolphino will be able to breathe there, maneuver himself around, and have new food sources to live life easily.

So, on the night of the annual *Shooting Stars Meteor Shower*, Jesse, Chaz, and Dolphino leave Earth to begin their *new adventure* to save the planet Plethoria. . .and possibly Earth!

CHAPTER 17

Exploring Mystery Mountain

FTER THEY ARRIVE SAFELY and secretly on Plethoria, Sandor has made plans to hide them in a cave near Mystery Mountain, where the Sacred Spaceship is encased. As they approach the cave, Astrid comes running out sobbing and waving her arms. Both mother and father embrace Jesse and then Chaz. *They cannot believe, after all these years, they are finally holding their two sons.* Zee also rushes out to meet Chaz and to embrace Jesse. When the boys and Dolphino are settled in (and you can well imagine what a shock it is for his parents and friends to see a dolphin with them),

Father details Murado's evil plan. Murado is getting ready to activate the dreaded Drago X2 and then capture all the remaining people of Plethoria.

He then plans to capture Chaz, destroy or maybe just torture him, and enslave him for life in the mines. He calls this "Giving you, Chaz, a *new grand prize!*"

Now the boys know they have to do *something* to save Nanney, Lani, and all of the people on the other planets, including, of course, their own, first.

THE NEXT DAY JESSE AND CHAZ EXPLORE Mystery Mountain and the *sacred spacecraft*, hoping to unlock its ancient secret.

As they approach the mountain, they are dumbfounded by the size of the craft and puzzled that no one is guarding it. The boys assume, since so many others had tried and failed to activate the ship, that everybody simply thinks it's impossible.

But a strange feeling comes over them as they come closer, and they are drawn to an unusual hatchway. Reaching out, Jesse stumbles and grabs onto the handle of the door to break his fall. To his utter astonishment, the hatch begins to open, revealing a magnificent cockpit with three seats and a huge, sophisticated control panel. The boys immediately begin to explore this wonder.

If only they can unlock its secret! *Wait!* Maybe they *do* have a chance, as they are almost magically invited into the craft. Something draws them to a very special section of the control panel. They think it is strange there are two odd-shaped openings on the panel.

Chaz murmurs, "Where have I seen this shape? It looks so *familiar.*"

"Chaz, Chaz! It's the same shape as our *pendants!*"

Could *this* be the *special secret* no one has been able to discover? Could these two boys be the ones to save the planet? Are the pendants the keys to activate the ship?

They nervously, in complete silence, unhook the pendants from their necklaces. Finally, Jesse whispers, "Okay—on the count of three, we'll then insert the pendants. Ready? Okay, then. One. . .two. . .*three!*" They slide the pendants into the openings on the control panel, and, instantly, the engine comes to life with a great roar! The ship begins to rock back and forth. The whole panel lights up like fireworks on the Fourth of July, and a strange voice calls out, "On the count of ten, start ignition!"

"Wait!" Jesse screams. "We're not ready to go. Take out the pendants! But. . .but we've unlocked the secret!" They remove the pendants, and he adds, "Let's go home and make preparations to come back, take off, and challenge Murado. Brother, *we* have been chosen, by some strange force, to operate this ship. Now I *know* we will succeed!

CHAPTER 18

Challenging Murado

A S THE BOYS BREATHLESSLY APPROACH the cave to share the great news, they stop dead in their tracks! They can't believe their eyes, for there is Dolphino, out of his aquatic box, moving about and breathing as freely as they do. And, yes, the unique atmosphere of the planet has transformed Dolphino's DNA.

How wonderful! Now he can easily be their third pilot. Everything is quite mysteriously falling into place, as if some universal power has been controlling their destiny all along.

Word has gotten back to the family that Murado is

preparing to attack Plethoria in two days. The family knows they have no time to waste. The boys will have to leave on the same day and, once and for all, put an end to that evil creature, his followers, and their awful plans.

ON THE MORNING OF THEIR DEPARTURE, the whole population accompanies the boys and the dolphin to Mystery Mountain. They are astonished when Jesse touches the hatch door and it automatically opens. A hush falls over the group. Everyone knows that this is a life-or-death challenge, and that their lives all depend on the outcome! The boys' mother and father rush to hug them before they enter the ship. It is a very touching moment . . .and it may be their last ever together.

The three enter the ship, and the door closes behind them.

Inside, they seem instinctively to know what to do. Jesse and Chaz insert their pendants into the control panel. They strap themselves in. For one brief moment, the boys laugh out loud, for someone has given Dolphino a pair of goggles and a pilot's hat, which he proudly wears.

In a flash, the control panel is aglow with multi-colored lights. The engine starts to roar, and that strange voice starts counting down: "Ten, nine, eight, seven, six, five, four, three. . .two. . .one. . .*blast off!*"

It is a sight to behold! The spaceship slowly begins to rock back and forth and rise above Mystery Mountain. Father, Mother, and all the other witnesses give a roaring cheer. They then return to the cave and wait for news of the beloved boys and their companion. Zee tries to offer a few words of encouragement. He knows their task may—or may not—be successful, though he won't share this thought with anyone. But everyone knows, in their hearts, that it's true.

TRAVELING SO SWIFTLY THROUGH SPACE, it isn't long before they spot Murado in his menacing black-and-silver DragoX2. Dolphino begins to squeal out that he, too, has spotted the ship, and asks for his orders. At the same moment, they know that Murado has spotted them too—for he is turning his ship to face them.

Inside the DragoX2, Murado can't believe what he is seeing. Speeding directly at him is the sacred ship from the Mystery Mountain! But who—who could be piloting it? He clamps his teeth on the thought. Who could possibly have the power to remove it from that mountain?

Chaz makes radio contact with Murado's ship.

"That voice!" Murado exclaims. "That voice—I've heard it before! Why does that voice sound so familiar? . . . No, it couldn't *possibly* be him! He's still on *Earth!*"

He shouts into the radio, "Identify yourself!"

"Identify myself? You *know* who this is! It's Chaz. . . the very one who beat you in the Grand Race and who is going to *destroy* you now!

Murado laughs out loud, "You and who else?"

"Me, my brother Jesse, and a friend."

"Destroy *me?* Are you kidding me? You *fools!* I'm too powerful for you! Prepare to meet your end!"

Their ships are speeding toward each other—and Jesse realizes that Chaz knows *exactly* what he's thinking. "Have we come this far, only to fall so soon in battle? Oh, Mother and Father, I did so want to get to know you. What will become of you, of our people, and of all the beings in our universe? We can't lose. We just *can't!*"

Can you guess what happens next?

Murado, furious, begins to scream commands at his crew saying, "These fools don't know how powerful I am! Get the new Laser Smasher Beam ready to fire!"

Yes, this time *he* will be the winner and Chaz the loser. His Smasher Beam is aimed at the boys: Ready, aim, *fire. . . !*

But the boys' ship turns 360 degrees, and the beam just by-passes them. Murado, seeing that his beam has failed, purposely leads them into the asteroid belt. He maneuvers his ship so that one gigantic asteroid is speeding directly at the boys. They have no time to move out of its path! Suddenly, a light begins to flash on Jesse's control panel, illuminating one switch. He instinctively presses the button, and something amazing happens. Leg-like structures with feet pop out of the sides of the ship, and their ship climbs right *over* the asteroid!

The boys and Dolphino start screaming, yelling, high-fiving, and high-finning each other!

Murado screams at his crew to get the dreaded Green Mist Activator ready. At first, he thought he wanted to destroy the boys, but now he will capture and enslave them instead!

"All hands on deck!" he commands. "Ready, aim, *fire!*"

From the belly of his ship the weird green mist slithers forth. It rapidly approaches the boys' ship. Without speaking a word, they know they are doomed. They will be sucked up and captured.

But, again, they are stunned! Just before the mist encircles them, a side panel on their ship opens, and out pops a huge, strange-looking *hand* that *seizes* the mist and throws it back to the DragoX2. Instead of encircling them, the mist is sucked back into Murado's ship engines. Murado's plan *backfires*. His ship sputters, rocks back and forth, shakes violently, and *explodes!* Shattered pieces of the ship disappear into outer space, putting an end to the *evil reign of Murado!*

WHEN THE BOYS REACH HOME, they are given a hero's welcome. All of Plethoria is there to greet them. The Great One is there in person to bestow the Medal of Excellence on Jesse, Chaz, and Dolphino. The boys, and the dolphin, wave to the crowd amid boisterous cheers!

Mother, Father, and Zee come running through the crowd and embrace them all. What a sight! Because of the destruction of Murado, Jesse now knows he will start his new, exciting life safe from any evil element.

Jesse, Chaz, and Dolphino have saved the planet, the universe and, in Jesse's heart, just as important, have saved Nanney and Lani!

And, perhaps, someday, he will see them *again*.

Perhaps.

Perhaps. . . .

PERHAPS. . . .

ABOUT THE AUTHOR

Evelyn Rocco's personal life experiences, along with her elementary and middle-school teaching career in New Jersey, have provided her with many interesting, rewarding opportunities and experiences. They include conducting a teacher-training workshop, consulting for charter schools, and being listed in *Who's Who in American Education*.

Her educational background and personal life have enabled her to spend numerous hours enjoying fiction and non-fiction material, coupled with various hobbies and other activities. In time, she resolved to write a story that would really spark one's imagination.

The Night Of The Shooting Stars is a science-fiction tale that she hopes will appeal to children of all ages—and even adults who love stories in that genre like *Star Trek, Star Wars,* and *Avatar.*